# Bungalo Boys II

### By John Bianchi

## Bushmen Brouhaha

An orange glow from the morning sun burns the mist off the African savannah. High overhead in a small plane, the **Bungalo Boys** prepare to drop into the magic and mystery of the Serengeti.

On board the plane, the Bungalo Boys check their equipment one last time.

Curly makes sure his hair tonic is tightly capped. Johnny-Bob inspects his supply of tooth-care products. Ma Bungalo, the plane's pilot, helps Rufus secure the lid on a crate of supplies.

After playing hide-and-seek in the parachute, Little Shorty hastily repacks it in preparation for the big jump.

Rather than land the noisy plane, the boys have decided to hit the silk . . .

. . . so as not to disrupt the peaceful lives of the animals below.

Once on the ground, the Bungalo Boys
establish base camp Bravo Bravo.

During breakfast, Rufus wonders if they have
pitched their tent too close to one of the
Serengeti's many migration routes.

Later that morning, the wily Bungalo Boys approach some local bushmen. Though Johnny-Bob does not recognize their dialect, he is able to use Universal Bungalo Sign Language to engage them for the expedition.

# Some Universal Bungalo Sign Language:

"Bunny Rabbit"

"Walk"

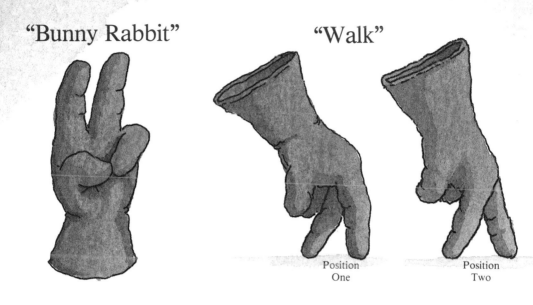

Position
One

Position
Two

"Hop"

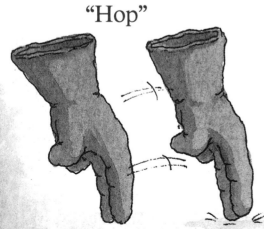

Position
One

Position
Two

"Do you
have a spare
banana?"

The bushmen help the boys track and capture an elusive Tanzanian elephant tree. In no time, the big-game tree ranchers have tamed the magnificent beast.

"Let's call her Buffy!" suggests Johnny-Bob.

With Projectile the wonder dog bounding ahead and the Bungalo Boys high atop Buffy the Tanzanian elephant tree, the Serengeti expedition is finally under way.

The bushmen follow closely behind, carrying the boys' equipment and singing rhythmic native songs. Already, Little Shorty is hungry.

The Bungalo Boys are gifted naturalists. They encounter many exotic animals and skillfully record their findings while leaving the beauty of the Serengti virtually undisturbed.

Little Shorty is left in charge of the bushmen. Within minutes, they are surrounded by a tribe of hungry blue-nosed baboons intent on feasting upon the bushmen's berries.

"What now, Little Bwana?" signs the head bushman nervously.

Little Shorty panics! In a mindless attempt to drive the baboons away, he lights a nearby branch.

"LITTLE BWANA GOT BANANA FOR BRAIN!!!" shouts the head bushman. "YOU TORCH BROTHER SABU! NOW WHOLE SAVANNAH GO UP IN SMOKE!!!"

The ensuing hubbub alerts the ever vigilant Bungalo Boys.

"Jumpin' Jack Pines!" shouts Curly, itching for a good scrap. "There's a bunch of baboons pickin' on the bushmen!!! Git that there pachyderm a snortful of water and climb aboard!"

Birds flutter from trees! Animals scatter wildly in all directions! The entire Serengeti trembles as the mighty Tanzanian elephant tree thunders down on the bushmen's brouhaha!

One blast from Buffy's massive honker douses the fire and sends the terrified blue-nosed baboons scrambling into the surrounding savannah.

With the brouhaha quelled, the Bungalo Boys head back to base camp Bravo Bravo. It has been a long day of adventure, and the boys look forward to some early shut-eye. Morning will come soon, and they have only begun to unravel the secrets of the Serengeti!